SKYSCRAPER BABIES

SKYSCRAPER BABIES

Words by
April Pulley Sayre and Jeff Sayre

Illustrated by
Juliet Menéndez

GODWINBOOKS

Henry Holt and Company
New York

Skyscraper babies
grow

high.
Close to their families.
Close to the sky.

HOMES may differ.

Ledges. Edges.
Old. New.
Cliffside condo,
or tree-trunk view.

Yet **BABIES** are **BABIES.**

Eyes closed, they rest.
They squirm and stretch
in nook or nest.

FAMILIES

fuss,

flap!

Nag,

nibble,

need.

Tend both ends!
Clean and feed!

PARENTS dash out.

Babies

COO,
CRY.

They squawk their sorrow to street and sky.

GROWN-UPS
& HELPERS

carry,   climb,   leap!

Change linens
and leaves.
SOOTHE
babies to sleep.

Skyscraper babies **HEAR** bellows and bells,

LEARN

voices and songs
and touches and smells.

Babies **GROW** bigger,

grow crowded at home.

It's time for fresh air.

Babies must

ROAM!

Some flap,
**FLY
FAR.**
Parents feed.
Parents follow.
Up, up, others climb.

RUN BACK

to their hollow.

Others
descend
to ground
or ground floor.
Babies' first wander!

It's time to EXPLORE!

Skyscraper babies
grow

high.
Close to their families.
Close to the sky.

APRIL PULLEY SAYRE

was a beloved, award-winning children's book author, a photo illustrator, a naturalist, and an accomplished wildlife photographer. She died in November 2021 after a long, valiant fight against metastatic breast cancer.

During her prolific career, she created eighty-two books, with her captivating photos illustrating fourteen of them. This book is one of three still in the works.

Her read-aloud nonfiction books are known for their lyricism and praised for their scientific precision. She was perhaps best known for pioneering literary ways to immerse young readers in natural events via creative storytelling and unusual perspectives.

"My work is about wonder and scientific inquiry," April once shared. "I try to communicate the excitement I feel about nature and my fascination with the way scientists discover how nature works."

April was an extraordinary human being who left behind a powerful and hopeful legacy. Through her words and photos, she painted a picture of the grandeur of the natural world and the importance of protecting it. Her unique insights and creative ways of exploring humanity's connections with the rest of nature will inspire readers for generations.

Learn more about April at aprilsayre.com.

Continuing April's Legacy

April and Jeff Sayre shared an immutable bond and a love of nature. Nature was the common thread that connected their lives. Together they spent thirty-three amazingly wonderful years exploring, communicating about, and working for the conservation of the natural world. To continue this legacy, they started the April & Jeff Sayre Fund for Nature, an officially recognized, tax-exempt nonprofit private foundation. Learn more at sayrenature.org.

Long before architects, engineers, and builders dreamed of and constructed the first city skyscrapers, some early humans lived in natural skyscrapers such as cliff dwellings and tree houses. These high perches provided a unique view of the surrounding landscape. They also provided shelter from the elements and protection from some dangers.

But humans are not the only animals that take advantage of the benefits offered by natural skyscrapers. A number of animal species roost and raise their young in cliffside residences or high up in trees.

Skyscraper Birds

Many bird species take advantage of skyscraper-like homes built by nature, such as trees or cliff ledges. But when living in the city, they may utilize skyscrapers and other structures built by people.

In the wild, peregrine falcons will nest high up on a cliff, but in the city, they will nest on the ledge of a tall building or on a bridge. Killdeer and common nighthawks select a sandy or gravelly spot on the ground when nesting in the wild. But when dwelling in the city, these two species prefer to nest on the pebbly rooftops of buildings.

Skyscraper Mammals

In city parks and backyards, northern raccoons seek out large cavities in trees to den and raise their babies. If they cannot find a suitable spot in a tree, they may resort to living underground in an abandoned burrow or living in a human-made structure such as a shed.

Eastern fox squirrels take advantage of tree cavities as well. If one is not available, they will construct a home up in a tree out of sticks and leaves. Their babies grow up in the protection offered by trees.

**These are only a few examples of wild skyscraper babies.
Visit aprilsayre.com to discover many more!**

Helping Skyscraper Babies

Whether living in cities or wild areas, all skyscraper babies require a safe and healthy habitat. Here are ways you can help.

1. Keep your cats indoors: Domestic cats are estimated to kill over 2 billion (yes, billion) birds each year in the United States. They also kill many small mammals, reptiles, and amphibians. Learn more at https://abcbirds.org/program/cats-indoors/.

2. Plant a pollinator garden: Providing sources of nectar for bees, wasps, and hummingbirds is important. The flowers will also attract insects that birds eat and produce seeds that some birds and mammals eat.

3. Reduce your lawn: Save time mowing by turning some of your lawn into a pollinator habitat, woodland, or prairie garden. Adding wild space to your yard will benefit a wide diversity of creatures.

4. Landscape with native plants: Include native plants in your landscaping design, especially trees and shrubs that produce edible fruit.

5. Encourage habitat protection: Many wetlands, prairies, forests, lakes, rivers, streams, canyons, and deserts are in decline. Local parks and private nature centers often have conservation initiatives to protect such habitats. Contact them to see how you can help.

6. Encourage your community to participate in Audubon's Lights Out program to protect birds during the few weeks in spring and fall when they are migrating. Learn more at https://www.audubon.org/lights-out-program.

7. Reduce or eliminate pesticide use.

8. Share your excitement with others: One of the best ways to help wild animals and encourage conservation is by sharing your knowledge and passion for nature with others.

Thank you, April Pulley Sayre,
for inspiring us all to look more closely
and delight in the world around us.
—J.M.

Henry Holt and Company, *Publishers since 1866*
Henry Holt® is a registered trademark of Macmillan Publishing Group, LLC
120 Broadway, New York, NY 10271 • mackids.com

Our books may be purchased in bulk for promotional, educational, or business use.
Please contact your local bookseller or the Macmillan Corporate and
Premium Sales Department at (800) 221-7945 ext. 5442 or
by email at MacmillanSpecialMarkets@macmillan.com.

Library of Congress Control Number: 2022920606

First edition, 2023
Book design by Juliet Menéndez
Illustrations are done using Old Holland watercolors on aquarelle arches paper and edited digitally.
Printed in China by RR Donnelley Asia Printing Solutions Ltd.,
Dongguan City, Guangdong Province

ISBN 978-1-250-13977-1 (hardcover)
1 3 5 7 9 10 8 6 4 2